Splash Dance

READ ALL THE SHARK SCHOOL BOOKS!

SHARK SCHOOL

#6 Splash Dance

BY DAVY OCEAN
ILLUSTRATED BY AARON BLECHA

ALADDIN   New York   London   Toronto   Sydney   New Delhi

WiTH THANKS TO PAUL EBBS

ALADDIN
An imprint of Simon & Schuster Children's Publishing Division
1230 Avenue of the Americas, New York, NY 10020
First Aladdin hardcover edition September 2015
Text and concept copyright © 2014 by Hothouse Fiction
Illustrations copyright © 2014 by Aaron Blecha
Originally published in 2014 in Great Britain as *Shark Party* by Templar Publishing.
Also available in an Aladdin paperback edition.
For information about special discounts for bulk purchases, please contact
Simon & Schuster Special Sales at 1-866-506-1949 or business@simonandschuster.com.
The Simon & Schuster Speakers Bureau can bring authors to your live event. For more
information or to book an event contact the Simon & Schuster Speakers Bureau at 1-866-248-3049
or visit our website at www.simonspeakers.com.
Jacket designed by Karin Paprocki
Interior designed by Mike Rosamilia
The text of this book was set in Write Demibd.
Manufactured in the United States of America 0715 FFG
2 4 6 8 10 9 7 5 3 1
Library of Congress Control Number 2015942098
ISBN 978-1-4814-0696-3 (hc)
ISBN 978-1-4814-0694-9 (pbk)
ISBN 978-1-4814-0697-0 (eBook)

CHAPTER 1

"*Moooooooooooooooooooooooooooom!*
Stop it! It's breakfast time. I want to eat
my breakfast. I want to enjoy my breakfast. I don't want to talk about exams!
I want to concentrate on breakfast.
Are you trying to give me fin-digestion
before I even start eating?"

I don't think Mom is listening. She's swimming around the kitchen, preparing breakfast on autopilot—sloooooooooooooow autopilot. There are kelp krispies popping and crackling in a bowl as they turn soggy (and kelp krispies are awful when they're mushy). And she hasn't even put the crab Pop-Tarts in the toaster yet! All she's interested in doing is going on and on about the Quay Stage 2 exams I have to take next month at school.

"Well, Harry, I know studying isn't your favorite pastime," Mom says for the third time as she swims right past the Pop-Tarts, "but it really is important . . ."

In my head I'm yawning. It's a BIG yawn. Not as big as the hungry hole in my tummy, but it's close.

Dad is no help at all. He's got his hammer head stuck in today's *Seaweed Times*, scanning the pages to see if there's anything about him. Dad's Mayor of Shark Point, and usually there's a picture of him in the paper, opening a new building, or kissing a newspawn, or standing next to an important visitor from another reef. He likes to cut the stories out and put them up on the wall of

his office. Today he doesn't seem to have found anything about himself. This always makes him grumpy.

"Dad," I say, "could you pass my kelp krispies, ple—?"

"Not one picture!" Dad slaps a fin against the paper. "I had a dozen photos taken yesterday and not a single one has made it into the paper. It's like I don't exist!" Dad does like to exaggerate when he gets upset. I've got to do something RIGHT NOW, so that:

1. Mom stops talking about exams.
2. Dad stops talking about himself.

3. My breakfast moves from the counter to my mouth before the rumbling in my tummy causes a seaquake!

And then I see it.

As Dad grumpily holds up the newspaper, I see an ad for the new Fintendo SeaWii-DS on the back.

Oh, WOW!

All the hunger is pushed from my tummy as I fin up close to the back page. Dad is still huffing and muttering behind it, but I don't care.

I'm too busy looking at the ad for the ultra-new fin-held game console, with SeaWii-DS graphics and Super Snapper Races 8. And it's out today.

I WANT ONE!!!!

"Now, about this studying . . . ," Mom says, finally putting the crab tarts in the toaster.

But I'm not listening, I'm reading all the mouthwatering specs in the ad:

1. SeaWii-DS Screen!
2. Depth-Charge Slider!
3. Circle Pad Canalog Control!

4. WiFi-sh Communication!

5. TONS OF OTHER GREAT THINGS THAT I DON'T REALLY UNDERSTAND BUT ARE PROBABLY THE BEST THINGS EVER IN THE FISHTORY OF THE SEAVERSE!!!

It all looks so cool.

"Mom!" I say, stabbing my fin so hard into the newspaper it goes right through and plonks Dad on the hammer. "Can I have one of these? Please, please? Pretty please with a side order of please?"

Dad looks at me angrily through the hole in the paper, and Mom catches the two crab tarts as they pop out of the toaster. "No!" they both say at exactly the same time, like they've been practicing.

"Why?" I ask, cutting around the ad with my fin so that I can stick it on my wall.

"Because it's bad for you," Mom says, finally bringing my breakfast over.

BAD FOR ME?!

I stare at her so hard my eyes nearly pop out of my hammer. What is wrong with her? How can something so good be bad?!

"You should be out playing with your friends, not stuck at home playing a silly

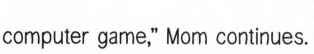

computer game," Mom continues.

SILLY?! I'm starting to think Mom might actually have gone crazy.

"But, Mom, I'd have way more friends to play with if I had one of these. I'd be the most popular shark in Shark Point!"

But Mom just shakes her head. "There's no way I'm changing my mind, Harry. Anyway, you should be concentrating on your studying at the moment."

I can't believe she's being so mean! I'm her son. Her only son. Doesn't my happiness mean anything to her?

"I have rights, you know!" I say, puffing up my chest and sticking out my dorsal fin.

Mom looks at me like I've just broken her best vase with a finball.

"I do! I'll list them for you if you don't believe me."

Mom stares at me. "Go on, then."

"Oh, well, uh, number one: I have the right to—uh—to develop proper fin—eye coordination!"

Mom just rolls her eyes.

"Number two: I—uh—uh—I have the right to express myself through getting the highest score at Super Snapper Races 8!"

Mom starts tapping her fin on the counter.

"Number three: I have the right to new technology. I should not be left behind in the backwater of old stuff where all you old sharks live!" (I think I might be going too far, but I can't seem to stop now . . .)

TAP
TAP
TAP

"Number four: I have the right to have parents who love

me enough to give me what I need to become a happy and healthy hammer-head shark!"

The kitchen is silent, except for a few pops and crackles as the last of my kelp krispies finally turn to mush. Mom is glaring so hard at me I turn to Dad.

"Tell her, Dad—I need a Fintendo, don't I?"

Dad peers over the top of the paper, but he isn't looking at me, he's looking at Mom. "Harry, you definitely need something . . ." he says.

Yayyyyyyyyyyyyy!

"You need to be grounded for a week and get no fin money for a month if you don't apologize for upsetting your mom, right now!"

Oh.

Mom looks really angry. She snatches the ad from my fin, crumples it up, and throws it into the trash can.

"Now, you listen to me, Harry," she says. "If you don't start studying and pass your exams, not only will you *not* be getting a Fintendo, but you won't be going to the end-of-year party either!"

Mom takes my breakfast (I hadn't even

13

started eating it!) and throws the bowl in the dishwasher. Then she crosses her fins and stares at me.

I don't believe it. No Fintendo. No breakfast. And the threat of no end-of-school party!

THIS IS SO UNFAIR.

I bang my hammer on the table. "I can't believe how mean you're being. You're lucky I don't report you to the National Society for the Prevention of Cruelty to Hammerheads!"

With that, I storm out of the kitchen and swim to my bedroom as fast as my tail will propel me.

I throw myself onto my bed and pound the seaweed blanket with my fins.

"What's up, Harry?" Humphrey, my humming-fish alarm clock, says. Lenny the lantern fish (my bedside lamp) lights up and shines his glow on me.

"I am never, ever, ever, as long as I live, getting out of bed again," I wail, burrowing under the covers. "I am now the prisoner of the most evil dictator in the fishtory of shark-kind."

"Who's that?" asks Lenny.

"MY MOM!!!!!!!!!" I shout from under the covers. "She doesn't care about my happiness. All she wants me to do

15

is study, study, study—and she knows how much I hate studying. She is so evil she makes the sting of sting-rays feel like tickles, and the chomp of a great white feel like a kiss from your granny!"

"I think I'd rather be chomped by a great white," says Humphrey. "My granny smells like boiled sea cabbage and has lips like a sea cow's rear end."

"Whatever!" I whine, sticking an eye out from under the cover. "My mom's evil, evil Mrs. McEvil from Evilville-on-Sea!"

Just then Mom swims into the room, carrying my lunch box and a tray. The tray contains a bowl of fresh kelp krispies and a plate of crab Pop-Tarts.

"I'm sorry I shouted at you, Harry, but you did make me very angry," Mom says. "Now make sure you have a big breakfast. You want to have plenty of energy for your schoolwork." She puts the tray down beside my bed and tucks my lunch box into my backpack. "I've put an extra bag of krilled chips in your lunch box so you don't go hungry during the day."

"Wow," Humphrey says as Mom swims out of the room. "That sounds like the most evil breakfast and lunch box ever. What an evil dictator your mom is!"

Humphrey and Lenny start to snicker behind their fins.

"It's just an act!" I shout. "She *is* evil! You didn't hear what she said to me in the kitchen." But Humphrey and Lenny

are now floating on their backs, sur-
rounded by giggle bubbles.

"Hey, Harry," says a voice at the window. I look up and see my best friends—
Ralph the pilot fish, Joe the jellyfish, and
Tony the tiger shark—crowded at the
windowsill. "Want a game of finball before
school?" Ralph says with a grin. Tony
heads a ball toward Joe, who clutches it
in twelve of his legs, then uses a massive toot to aim it at my bedroom window.
I dive out of bed and flick it away with
my tail.

Saved!

I grab my backpack and a finful of

crab Pop-Tarts and head for the window.

"I thought you were never getting out of bed again!" Humphrey calls after me. He and Lenny start laughing their heads off again as I swim away.

By the time I get to the park, I've calmed down a bit, but then we hear a crowd approaching.

"Wow!"

"WOW!!"

"WOW WOW WOW!!!"

"WOW!!! WOW!!! WOW!!! WOW!!!"

A stream of our class friends come

through the park gates, flapping their fins in excitement.

"What's going on?" Tony says, swimming above us to get a better look. I push up to join him. They're all crowded around the broad back of a young bull shark.

"It's Billy," says Ralph, swimming up with Joe. "What's he holding?"

The other kids are all looking at something Billy has in his fins. I turn on my hammer-vision and use it to zoom in on the center of the crowd.

My stomach flips.

Billy is holding a new Fintendo SeaWii-DS!

21

He's playing Super Snapper Races 8 like a pro. His fins are flying across the controls and his eyes are fixed on the screen. I click off my hammer-vision and kick down toward him. I have to get a closer look at the console. Billy must have the best parents ever if they've

bought him a Fintendo on the day it comes out!

Ralph and the others follow me as I shoulder my way through the crowd.

When I finally catch a glimpse of it, I can't believe my eyes. It's as shiny as a black sea crystal and buzzing with noise and color. It looks even better in real life than it does in the ad. Billy finishes the level he's on and hits a new high score.

The crowd goes wild!

I push up to him. "Billy, your Fintendo's awesome! Can I try?"

Billy looks up from the console and

glares at me. "No way! I'm not lending this to anyone." He swims off toward the park gates.

The crowd moves on, following Billy like he's the coolest thing in the whole ocean.

It's so unfair! How come Billy gets a Fintendo and I don't? It's official—I have the evilest mom in the ocean!

CHAPTER 2

I don't feel any better by the time school starts, and my mood is not helped by our sea-turtle teacher, Mrs. Shelby. She keeps droning on and on about studying for our exams. It's like being at home with Mom!

How do they expect me to think about exams now that I've actually seen a new

Fintendo? I stare out of the window at the girls playing flounder ball. I'm not really that interested, but it's certainly more interesting than Mrs. Shelby's fishtory review.

"*Harry!*"

I jump as Mrs. Shelby yells at me.

"Yes, Mrs. Shelby?"

"Do you think you can tell me about King Moby the Eighth's first wife, Harry?"

"His first wife was called Harry?" I say without thinking. My cheeks start to turn red as I realize the silly mistake I've made.

"No, Harry," Mrs. Shelby continues, looking irritated. "Can you tell me her actual name?"

Ralph, who's at the desk next to me, whispers the answer into my ear. I turn back to Mrs. Shelby. "His first wife was called Catherine of Plankton."

Mrs. Shelby narrows her sea-turtle eyes. "Correct. And what happened to her?"

I sneak a look at Ralph, who shrugs. I look across the room and see Joe, who pretends to scratch his head with some of his tentacles so Mrs. Shelby can't see his face.

"I don't know," Joe mouths unhelpfully. Great!

I can hear Rick Reef and his side-kick Donny Dogfish snickering at me from the back of the room. My hammer is turning pinker than a prawnburger.

Mrs. Shelby sighs, and points back at the interactive whitebait-board. "For the benefit of Harry—and anyone else who wasn't listening—Moby the Eighth was King of Fingland from 1509 to 1547. He had six wives—Catherine of Plankton, whom he divorced; Anne Boatlyn, whom he had beheaded; Jane Seamour, who died giving birth to Moby's only son, Seaweed—who lived until he was just sixteen."

I bet King Moby wouldn't have put up with not having a Fintendo. He always seemed to get what he wanted.

"Then came Anne of Waves," Mrs. Shelby continues, "whom Moby divorced because he didn't like how she looked.

After Anne, Moby married Catherine
Sea-Coward, whom hated Moby so much
that she had lots of other boyfriends—so
Moby had her beheaded too."

Moby is sounding pretty evil by now—
not as evil as my mom, but getting there.

"Last, Moby married Catherine Starfish.

Unfortunately, they also had no children, but stayed married until Moby died in 1547, leaving his only living child, Elobsterbeth, to become Queen."

I look around the class. It turns out that everyone else, even Rick and Donny, have been writing all this down. I haven't written

a word. I've been too busy being annoyed at Mom and comparing her to Moby the Eighth. I lean over to Ralph to ask him if I can copy his notes later—but before I can say a word, the bell rings for recess.

"*Wait, please!*" Mrs. Shelby shouts as everyone starts getting up from their desks. "Before you go, I have an important announcement to make about the end-of-year party."

Everyone stops dead and listens. The end-of-year party is the best thing about school. Which makes Mom double-evil for threatening to not let me go. Mrs. Shelby pushes her little round glasses up her flat turtle face. "In fact, I have some very exciting news about the party."

We all stare at her, wide-eyed and openmouthed. What could it be?

"This year," Mrs. Shelby announces grandly, "there will be a competition to find the best dancer in the whole school!"

Is that it? I thought she said it was going to be EXCITING news. There's nothing exciting about danc-ing. All the boys start to groan. But the dolphin twins, Pearl and Cora, start

swimming around with glee, high-finning and whooping. I don't know why they're so happy. Dancing is dorky, and I can make a list to prove it. Dancing is stupid because:

1. Anyone doing it looks like they're desperate to go to the bathroom.

2. The only kids interested in dancing are girls, and who wants to look like a girl?!

3. The only other underwater creatures who enjoy dancing are SEA SPONGES who have nothing better to do on a Saturday night than watch *Dancing with the Starfish*.

4. Seriously. Isn't that enough to put anyone off dancing FOR LIFE???

While I've been making my ultra-important list, Mrs. Shelby has been making one of her own—listing all the reasons why dancing is great! Things like it's really good exercise, it's a great way of making friends, and it's so much fun. I can hardly believe my ears. Is she crazy?!

"And finally," Mrs. Shelby says, her voice all squeaky with excitement, "whoever comes in first in the end-of-year dance contest will win a special prize!"

Hmmm, I wonder what that will be? A pink sparkly leotard and glittery fin warmers?

"The dancer with the best routine,"

Mrs. Shelby says, "will win a brand-new Fintendo SeaWii-DS!"

OMC! (Oh. My. Cod.)

I'm so shocked, my hammer head actually hits the desk. Mrs. Shelby looks at me all worried.

I pick my face up and try to make my mouth speak, but it's not easy. "W . . . wh . . . what did you say, Mrs. Shelby?"

Mrs. Shelby shakes her head. "Oh, Harry, I'm going to have to have a word with your parents. You haven't listened to a word I've said all this time!"

"No—no—NO, Mrs. Shelby. I was listening . . . I'm just not sure I heard that

last part right. Could you say it again?"

Mrs. Shelby gives a big sigh. "I said that the student who does the best dance routine of the contest will win a brand-new Fintendo SeaWii-DS."

"That's what I thought," I say, and then

everything becomes a big blur. All I can think about is the prize.

"Are you all right, Harry?" Tony says as we swim out to the playground.

An actual Fintendo!

"Open your mouth,

Harry, I need a break-time snack," Ralph says.

A brand new Fintendo—for free!

I look around. Pearl and Cora have already taken over a corner of the playground and are busy practicing their ballet moves.

"You sure you're all right, pal?" Ralph asks.

I nod. "Never better! Want to know why?"

Ralph's eyes widen hopefully. "Because you're going to let me snack on your leftover crab Pop-Tarts?"

I shake my head. "No. Because I'm

going to win a Fintendo and it's going to be the easiest thing EVER!"

"You're going to dance?" Ralph laughs as I start flexing my fins and limbering up my hammer.

"You've always said dancing was dumb," says Joe. Purple flashes of confusion start running up and down his tentacles.

"Dancing *is* dumb," I say with a smile. "And that's exactly why I'm going to win!"

Joe's whole body starts flashing purple. "But . . . "

FLUBBBBBBERRRRRRRRR!!!!

Suddenly my head is shaking and the

world looks like it's made of quivering rubber.

I hear Rick snickering behind me. He's sneaked up and *boinged* my hammer. Ralph and Joe catch hold of each end of my head to try to stop it from flubbering.

"You? Dance?" Rick sneers. "You couldn't dance your way out of a dead clam!"

"I-I-I . . . can . . . d-d-d-dance!" I stammer. My voice is all over the place—I sound like a Super Mario Carp backfiring on the starting grid.

As my flubbering head slows down,

Rick's pointy face comes into focus. He leans right into my hammer, his nose stuck between my eyes.

"That Fintendo is mine, Harry, and no goofy little stammerhead is going to get in my way!"

CHAPTER 3

I spend the rest of the day hardly able to concentrate on anything. When the final bell rings I zoom out of school, leaving Ralph and the others behind in a cloud of *WHOOSH!!!* I don't think I've ever gotten home so quickly.

I hardly notice the delicious smell of

freshly baked fish cakes coming from the kitchen. I fly up the stairs and hook my tail on the top banister to swing me around the coral corridor at insane speed.

"Harry, is that you? Do you want a fish c—?" is all I hear from Mom before I slam the door behind me, head for my desktop P-Sea, and flick it on.

I need to surf the interwet, and I need to surf the interwet NOW.

Humphrey and Lenny float toward me and start looking over my shoulder.

"You still sulking, Harry?" Humphrey asks as the P-Sea boots up.

"Oh no! What's that smell?" Lenny says, stifling a giggle. "Could it be your evil dictator mom making some deadly fish cakes? Shall we inform the authorities?"

"No, thank you," I tell them calmly.

The screen flickers to life. I do a quick search for the site I need. . . .

"'The Life and Times of Moby the Eighth'?" Lenny reads. "Harry, what are you doing?"

"Studying, of course," I tell them.

"But you hate studying!" Lenny exclaims, his light blinking.

"Not anymore," I say.

"But . . . ," says Humphrey.

"I don't understand . . . ," says Lenny.

I sigh and turn to look at them. "If I don't study, I won't pass my exams, and if I don't pass my exams, I can't go to the end-of-year party, and if I can't go to the end-of-year party, I won't be able to enter the dance competition, and if I can't enter the dance competition—"

"You won't turn into a girl?" says Humphrey.

"No," I say. "If I can't enter the dance competition, then I can't win the dance competition, and if I can't win the dance competition, I can't swim

away with a new Fintendo SeaWii-DS.
And I REALLY want a new Fintendo
SeaWii-DS. Now can you please be
quiet? I have a ton of catching up to
do!"

I turn back to the screen and start
to read.

I wake up the next morning with my head on the P-Sea's keyboard and my chin covered in sleepy drool.

I must have fallen asleep studying.

I stretch my aching body and head downstairs. It's Saturday, so I'll have plenty of time to study once I'm feeling a bit more awake. Dad comes swimming out of the kitchen with a finful of shrimp Pop-Tarts. I grab a couple for breakfast and look at Dad with my best hopeful goggly eyes.

Dad sighs and digs into his pocket.

He brings out but-
tons, an old, rusty
key, some coral
marbles, and (finally!)
his wallet.

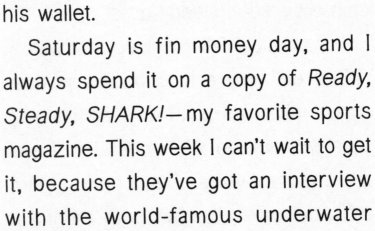

Saturday is fin money day, and I always spend it on a copy of *Ready, Steady, SHARK!*—my favorite sports magazine. This week I can't wait to get it, because they've got an interview with the world-famous underwater sharklete Turbo Tex.

"Are you all right, Harry?" Dad says as he hands me my money. "You look really tired."

"Oh, I was just up late studying," I say casually.

Dad's eyes widen in surprise. "Really?"

I nod.

"Well, that's very good to hear. Very good indeed." He slaps me on the back. "Keep at it and one day you might even be as clever as me!"

"That would be cool, Dad!" I say with a grin.

After quickly eating my Pop-Tarts I head out to Shark Point. The water is still cool, but I hardly notice. One half of my mind is on Turbo Tex, and the other is on the Fintendo I'm going to win at the end of the year. Then, suddenly, I hear a girl's voice.

"No, you should do a tail-twist with an overkick."

I look around and see Pearl and Cora on the opposite side of the street. They've got their bags over their shoulders and they're wearing sparkly pink fin warmers. They're so deep in conversation they don't even notice me.

"Then I'll do a plié, followed by a pirouette," Cora says.

A WHAT followed by a WHAT?

"Ooh, yes," says Pearl. "That would

be perfect! We are so going to win this dance competition!"

The girls high-fin and keep going down the street. So they were talking about dancing. Hmmm. This gives me an idea. Maybe they're going off to practice somewhere. I could spy on them and see if I can get a few tips for my own routine.

I drift over to the shadows at the edge of the street and start following them. I don't need to worry about being seen, though—they're way too busy talking about their own moves.

I follow the twins all the way to a

building on the outskirts of town. They swim up some rickety old stairs and disappear inside. I hear the faint sound of a piano playing. I've come too far to turn back now—if I'm going to learn a few dance moves from the girls, I'm going to have to look inside.

I creep up the stairs. As I reach the door at the top, the music gets louder, and I can hear the swishing of several tails. The door isn't completely shut, so I float up close to it and place a goggly eye by the gap. It takes a few seconds for my eye to adjust to the bright lights inside. The wall opposite me is covered with mirror-carp scales. A sign at the top of the wall reads:

MADAME L'OCTOPUS'S BALLET STUDIO

Ballet!

I'm not doing any ballet in my dance routine—that's way too girly.

Pearl and Cora have joined a group of girl fish and dolphins. They're all dressed in pink ballet gear and they're warming up to the music.

There's nothing useful for me here. I start to swim away. But suddenly a thick, rubbery octo-pus tentacle shoots

through the door and grabs me by the tail!

I'm hauled into the room with a *thud*, and suddenly there's a huge greeny-pink face staring into mine. A high-pitched voice with a Trench accent screams in my ear.

"And what do we 'ave 'ere?"

"Harry!" Pearl yells.

"It's Harry Hammer, Madame L'Octopus," Cora says. "He goes to our school."

Madame L'Octopus stares at me. "And he is a ballet dancer, *oui*?"

"Well, I know he's good at dancing," Pearl says.

I stare at her in shock.

Pearl grins back at me. "Because he's

been telling everyone he's going to win the school dance competition."

"Veeery interesting," says Madame L'Octopus, waving me around in her huge tentacle. "Eet is about time we had a boy in this class. Let us see what the leetle dancey hammerhead can do."

The girls all giggle and start to clap along with the music. Madame L'Octopus lets go of me, but I can't escape. She's standing right between me and the door.

I'm trapped.

I can feel my face turning pink. I can't let Pearl and Cora see that I know

nothing about dancing. They'll tell Rick and I'll be the laughingstock of the school—again!

I think back to what I overheard the twins talking about on the way here. What was it? Pliers? Piro-nets? I have no idea what those moves are, but I have to do something. So I start waving my tail in time to the music and nodding my hammer backward and forward.

"I do believe 'ee can do ballet!" Madame L'Octopus cries, twirling around in a cloud of ink and rippling her tentacles with joy.

Hmmm, maybe this isn't going to be

so difficult after all. Feeling a bit braver,
I try to speed up. But then . . .

1. The girls form a circle around me, beating
   their fins in time.

2. I attempt a piro-net on my tail end (even
   though I don't actually know what that is)
   and clatter into a young hermit crab.

3. The hermit crab spins into Madame
   L'Octopus's mouth and causes her to have
   a coughing fit.

4. The coughing fit makes Madame L'Octopus
   squirt out a huge cloud of ink.

5. And suddenly no one can see where they
   are or where they're going.

6. And I crash into about ten girls.

7. And I end up with my hammer covered in mirror-carp scales, a pink fin warmer on my dorsal, and someone's frilly ballet skirt on my head!

As the ink clears, Cora and Pearl swim right up in front of me with their SeaBerry

smartphones—and start taking pictures!

"Oh my cod! Everyone's gonna love this on Plaicebook!" Pearl shrieks.

Disaster!

"*You!*" Madame L'Octopus shrieks, pointing all of her eight tentacles at me. "*You!!!*"

"Me, what?" I say, pulling the skirt off my head.

"You have ruined my mirror!"

We all turn to look at the far wall. The mirror-carp scales have all gone. Everyone looks back at me. The mirror-carp scales are now covering my skin. Some of the girls start checking their reflection in me! As fast as I can, I start flicking the scales off with my tail.

"You have to pay!" Madame L'Octopus yells, wrapping one of her tentacles around me. "You must pay for zee damage!"

"But—but . . . ," I stammer.

"But what?" she hisses.

"But I don't have any money," I reply. "Well, only my fin money . . ."

"Zat will do!" she snaps.

I stare at her.

She glares back.

"Give eet to me, then!"

Pearl and Cora start fiddling with their phones, ready to take another picture of

me. I quickly take my fin money out of my pocket and give it to her.

"Now go!" Madame L'Octopus yells.

If she wasn't so scary, I'd yell back, "Don't worry, I'm gone!" But she is scary—very scary—so I don't say a word and just swim for the door.

As soon as I get outside, I bang my hammer against the wall in despair. It's so unfair! I didn't even want to go to a dorky ballet class. I only came out to get a copy of *Ready, Steady, SHARK!*—and now I can't afford it!

I am totally fed up and completely broke. I brush the rest of the mirror-carp scales off me and start swimming home.

"Wow! You're so miserable you look like you've been given turtle-toe jam for lunch!" a girl's voice says as I turn the corner.

Brilliant. Another girl who wants to make fun of me.

Could today get any worse?

CHAPTER 4

I spin around, thinking it might be one of the girls from the ballet class. But it isn't.

A young leopard shark swims in front of me. She's wearing a cool Pike tracksuit. Her cap is on back-to-front and her neck is dripping with shipwreck bling.

"So, what's up?" she asks, giving me a fin bump. "Why you lookin' so stressed? I'm Lola, by the way. And you're Harry Hammer, aren't you?"

I look at her, confused. "Yeah—uh—how do you know?"

Lola grins. "Seen you with your dad in the newspapers."

"Oh." I'm not sure if she's about to make fun of me, so I don't smile back.

"It's all right. I don't bite," Lola says. "Just saw you looking all grumpy, so I

thought I'd see what the matter was. You don't have to tell me if you don't want to, though."

Lola's smile looks friendly, so I explain what happened back at the ballet school, and about the competition and the Fintendo prize.

Lola snorts with laughter, but it's not mean like Rick's—it's much more sympathetic.

"So you want to learn to dance?"

I nod.

"Well, you're not going to learn how to win the competition at ballet school. Ballet's really boring, isn't it?"

"I suppose."

"Real dancing's learned on the street."

I frown. "What do you mean?"

Lola starts spinning on the spot before doing a backflip and a star-fin. "See?" she says with a smile. "Want me to show you how?"

Suddenly I feel a million times better. "Yes, please!"

Lola nods. "Let's go to the skate park. I'll have you break-dancing in no time!"

"Oh . . . I . . . I can't go there."

Lola puts her fins on her hips and frowns at me. "Why not?"

"Well—uh—my mom says I'm not

allowed over there." I feel my face start to burn.

Lola shakes her head. "Are you some kind of mama's shark? Maybe I should just take you back to ballet class, then!"

"No!" I yell. "I want to learn how to break-dance and I don't care where I have to go to do it. I've got to win that Fintendo!"

Lola zooms past me, barrel-rolling into a skimming rush right past my hammer. Then she flicks out her fins and finishes with her tail bent up and her fins thrown back. It's the most brilliant dance move I've ever seen. "You sure

you want to dance like this, Harry? It's not for mama's sharks, you know!"

Right now I want nothing more than for Lola to show me how to dance. She is one of the coolest sharks I have EVER met!

I nod again, this time totally sure.

"Come on, then!"

And *BANG!* She's off like a rocket.

We shoot down narrow alleys and through dark, dingy streets, heading toward South Central Shark Point. I've never been to this part of Shark Point before. The walls are covered in graffiti and there are no houses, just coral buildings and chain-link fences. We head past a load of closed-down shops and a row of empty factories. The fish and sharks around us seem bigger and scarier than the ones I'm used to. I can hear police sirens not too far away, and whale trains thunder

overhead, dragging cargoes of ship-wreck metal.

Eventually we come to the skate park. Behind rusty fences, the park is alive with sharks of all shapes and sizes. All of them are wearing Pike or FishHead sports gear. A gang of leopard sharks are riding yellow-finned skateboards.

"All right, Leon!" Lola calls to the nearest leopard shark. He looks around and jumps off his skateboard. Then he waves a fin to the others, and one by one the group coasts to a halt, looking at me suspiciously.

Lola looks back at me. "Harry, this is

my dance crew—the Shark Beatz." Lola turns back to the gang. "Don't worry, boys, this is Harry. He's cool."

The Shark Beatz don't seem so sure, though. Leon flicks his tail over and stares at me with narrow eyes. "He doesn't look that cool to me."

"I told you, he's all right." Lola turns to me. "This is Leon.

He's my brother, and he's not as mean as he thinks he is."

Leon frowns, but doesn't say anything. He doesn't stop staring at me, though.

Lola beckons me forward with her fin. "Harry wants to learn how to dance. I brought him here so we could show him how to bust some moves."

The Shark Beatz start to laugh out loud. Leon cracks a huge smile. "A hammerhead? Dance? Do me a favor. All hammerheads are good for is knocking ships' nails into timber."

Lola nudges Leon. "Clam it. He needs our help, and we're going to give it to him, okay?"

I look at Lola. I'm not used to someone sticking up for me like this. It's making me feel a bit funny. I really hope it's not showing on my face. I stretch up to my full height. "Lola says you guys are the best dancers in all of Shark Point."

They nod.

"Well, I want to learn from the best."

This seems to do the trick, as the group all put their skateboards aside and form a circle around us.

Leon takes his phone from his pocket and starts playing a really cool ship-hop tune.

Lola starts flicking her tail back and forth to the beat. "Let's start with the most basic move—the Six Tail."

Lola and Leon go down on their bent tails, flicking them around in a circle and balancing their bodies on their fins behind them. They do six complete circles, then stop and stare at me.

"Go, Hammer!" Leon calls.

I start to bend my tail, trip over it, and smash my hammer in the worst self-*FLUBBERRRRRRRRRRRR* of all time.

Great.

My boinging head flubbers back and forth, and when it finally stops, Leon and the rest of the Shark Beatz are floating on their backs, holding their stomachs, laughing. I try the Six Tail again. This time I bend, circle, fin-balance, and *CRASH*.

Lola offers me a fin. "This might take

longer than I thought," she says kindly as she pulls me back up.

Over the next couple of hours, the Shark Beatz show me how to do all of their best moves:

1. The Catfish Daddy (all loose fins and wobbly head).

2. The Treasure-Chest Pop (waves through the chest and a dorsal slap).

3. The Plop, Rock, and Drop (a combination of a tail-plop, a body-rock, and falling over—I do the falling over part REALLY well. I'm just terrible at catching myself on my fins).

4. The Hammer-Dock (they made that one up especially for me). And then it's time for the hardest move of all . . .

5. The Head-Spin!

Lola turns herself upside down and, with a flick of her fins, starts to rotate on her head. She gets faster and faster as Leon and the Shark Beatz cheer her on. She whirs and blurs until I can't see her because she's moving so fast. Then *BANG!* She storms to a stop, fins out, tail flicked up to her dorsal, hanging there like the most rad thing of all time.

We all start cheering. But almost immediately I feel gloomy.

How can I ever do anything as good as that?

"Your turn, Hammer!" Lola calls as all of the Shark Beatz swim up to her, finning her on the back.

"Okay!" I shout, and flip myself upside down.

I flick out with my fins. Because of my big, flubbery hammer, it takes a lot more work to get myself moving than it does a sleek and beautiful leopard shark like Lola, but eventually I start to spin.

79

The whole world starts to revolve as I flick and kick.

Kick and flick.

As I get faster, it's easier and easier to move through the water. The skate park becomes spinning streaks of color . . .

I'm doing it.

I'm doing the hardest ship-hop move of all time.

The Head-Spin!

I'm amazing!

I'm awesome!

I'm a DANCER!

I'M A DANCER!!!

Even the Shark Beatz are cheering me

on. They're cheering and cheering and . . .

And . . . actually . . . it doesn't sound that much like cheering . . .

It sounds more like . . .

SCREAMING.

BOOOOOOOSH! I crash out of the Head-Spin and bounce onto the coral floor with a painful crunch.

I look up dizzily.

Everyone is spinning around me as if I'm still in the Head-Spin. But I can feel the rough coral against my back. It's NOT ME who's spinning.

IT'S THEM!

Then I realize what's happened . . .

My ridiculous hammer is so big, I've created an enormous whirlpool in the middle of the skate park!

Everyone is tumbling head over tail around me like socks in a washing machine. NOOOOOOOOOOOOOOOOOOOO!!!!!!!

Okay, I've messed up big-time.

I'm in a new place, throwing a group of tough sharks around like tadpoles in a sea tornado, and they are all screaming their heads off.

I am going to be in trouble so big, a word has yet to be invented for how GIGANTI-HUGE it's going to be. I cover my hammer with my fins and wait for the Shark Beatz to swim down and teach me a very painful lesson.

Except something I'm not expecting to happen happens. . . .

1. The screaming in the whirlpool starts to change.

2. The screams of fear become high-pitched screams of laughter.

3. As the whirlpool caused by my hammer starts to slow down, there's even more laughter.

4. I uncover my eyes and see the Shark Beatz holding on to one another and laughing.

5. And as they all slow down and gain control of their fins and tails, they start cheering!

6. Cheering ME!!!!

"Ham-MER! Ham-MER!! HAM-MERRRR-RRRRRRRR!!!!" they chant together. Leon has the widest smile on his face, and Lola swims down and hugs me tight in her fins! This makes me go all goggly-eyed.

"Wow, Harry, that was amazing!" Lola says. "That was the greatest Head-Spin we have ever seen. None of us have ever caused a whirlpool before!"

We all grab fins, touch tails, and dance around like clown fish in a carnival—madly whooping, high-finning, and generally laughing the teeth right out of our gums!

Even Leon comes over and shakes me by the fin. "Dude, I'm sorry I ever doubted you. You are going to be a totally radical dancer. You're FINtastic!"

And I *feel* FINtastic!

CHAPTER 5

It's the first day of the exams and we're all waiting for Mrs. Shelby to hand out our papers. At his desk across the room, Joe is turning a frightened shade of yellow. At the desk next to me, Ralph is trying to remember what happened to each of Moby the Eighth's wives.

"Divorced, beheaded, divorced—no, died," he mutters. "Divorced—or was that one beheaded?" He looks at Tony. Tony is staring into space and flicking his tail nervously. Even Rick looks uneasy as he chews on his pencil fish. But for the first time ever, I don't feel too bad about having to take an exam. Over the past few weeks I've spent more time studying than

I've spent eating kelp krispies—and that's a lot! And when I haven't been studying, or eating kelp krispies, I've been learning how to dance at the skate park with Lola. Now I feel ready to take on anything!

"Make sure you take your time with your answers," Mrs. Shelby says as she starts handing out the exams. "You don't want to make any silly mistakes."

I look down at the first question.

EXAM

What was King Moby's favorite sport?
a) Finball ☐
b) Flounder ball ☐
c) Hunting ☐

Hunting! I know because it came up when I was doing some last-minute reviewing this morning on my P-Sea.

I quickly check the answer. Then I read the next question.

What was the name of King Moby's daughter?
a) Seaweedia ☐
b) Elobsterbeth ☐
c) Crabella ☐

Yes! I know that one too—I learned it when I got Humphrey and Lenny

to pretend to be Moby's children the other day. It was partly to help me with my reviewing and partly to get back at them for teasing me about Mom not being evil.

I carefully check the Elobsterbeth box with my pencil fish. Then I go on to the next question.

What did King Moby wear on his head?
a) A starfish ☐
b) A jellyfish ☐
c) A crown fish ☐

Crown fish! And so it goes. Before I know it, I've finished the final question. I look around the classroom. The others are all still writing. I stare out the window and start going through my dance routine in my head. Thanks to Lola's teaching, my Catfish Daddy is going really well. I start wobbling my head and waving my fins as I imagine myself at the dance contest. The other contestants are all cheering, the judges are clapping their fins in time, and I'm—

"Harry! What are you doing?"

I jump in shock. Mrs. Shelby is floating next to my desk, glaring at me.

"Why are you wobbling your head? Why aren't you doing your exam?" she snaps.

"I've finished, Mrs. Shelby."

Mrs. Shelby sighs and shakes her head. "I told you not to rush, Harry. Rushing causes mistakes." She looks down at my paper. "Oh." She starts to smile as she reads through my answers. "Okay, well, just sit there quietly until the others have finished. No more head wobbling."

Head wobbling? Doesn't Mrs. Shelby know a Catfish Daddy when she sees one?! But I can't help grinning. Who'd have thought that studying would make exams almost fun?

The week of the exams goes by faster than a rocket fish. I get a bit muddled up in Trench and get some of my answers wrong in math, but mostly things go way better than normal. And the best thing is, Mom's so pleased with the way I studied that she's said I can go to the end-of-school party no matter what I get.

The day before the party, I go to the skate park for one last practice. Lola and Leon are there waiting for me. Lola's

holding some- thing for me in her fin.

"I got you this," she says, looking a bit embarrassed. "It's to bring you good luck at the dance contest."

She swims closer to me. She's holding a thick anchor chain decorated in shipwreck bling. It's almost as big as Leon's.

"Cool! Thanks," I say as she goes to put it on me. Luckily, it's big enough to fit over my hammer head.

"And I got you something too," Leon says with a grin. He hands me a baseball cap. It's got SHARK BEATZ studded in coral on the front.

"Wow!"

"Now you're really one of the crew," Lola says, grinning.

"What, really?" I say, my eyes goggling in shock.

"Yeah, bro," Leon says with a high fin. "You're our number one Head-Spinner."

"And you're going to win that dance contest for sure!" Lola

does a quick backflip. "Come on, let's go and practice some Hammer-Docks."

Lola and Leon head off to the middle of the park. As I swim after them, I feel like the happiest hammerhead alive. I've finished my exams and I'm allowed to go to the party. Now all I have to do is win the Fintendo!

And, for once in my life, I feel absolutely certain that nothing—and I mean NOTHING—can possibly go wrong.

CHAPTER 6

OH MY COD!

I've passed every exam I took with flying colors! Mrs. Shelby pats me on the head as I reread the results just to make sure. But it's true—I've come in first in almost everything! I am thirty-three tail flips and a shark smile happy!

Mom and Dad are just as excited when I get home from school and tell them the good news. We swim happy circles around the kitchen and knock a box of kelp krispies over. The krispies float through the water and start sticking to our skin. All three of us look like we've been covered in barnacles!

Then Dad shakes my fin. "Well done, son," he says, wiping a kelp krispie from his eye. "We're so proud of you."

"Yes we are!" says Mom, giving me a massive hug. "Well done, starfish! Now you can really enjoy the end-of-year party tonight."

I get a sudden fluttery feeling in my tummy.

Now that I've passed my exams, it's time for me to bag that Fintendo!

The school gym has been decorated for the end-of-year party. Well, when I say "decorated," what I mean is that a few strings of Christmas lights have been strung up and a huge glitter-pearl is hanging from the ceiling. A couple of really bored-looking lantern fish are taking turns to shine on it.

"I don't think much of the music," Joe mutters.

Ralph and Tony nod in agreement.

The DJ (also known as Mrs. Shelby) is playing some awful music from the olden days. They're songs my mom and dad like!

A table of snacks is set up against the far wall. Two rows of chairs line the

long walls on either side of the hall. One side has the boys sitting on them, the other has the girls. Each line is staring at the other, but not saying a word.

Pearl and Cora are in their ballet skirts and doing some dance moves. They must be warming up for the contest.

"Are you sure you're going to be able to beat them?" Ralph whispers.

I nod and grin. I haven't told my friends about my street-dancing lessons down at the skate park. I want it to be a surprise.

Then I see Rick and Donny over by the food table. They're tapping their fins to the music. Rick is all dressed up for the contest in his leather jacket and sunglasses. Well, he might look cool now, but seeing me dance will wipe that smirk off his face.

"Oh my cod! Look at that!" Ralph says, pointing a fin toward the dance floor.

Two ancient teachers—Mr. Kelp and Mrs. Clambury—are dancing together. Well, they're trying to dance together, but Mr. Kelp slips, pulls a fin, and has to be helped back to his chair.

It's all majorly embarrassing.

But I'm not really bothered. I'm here for one thing only, and that's the dance contest. I look at the clock, and my tummy churns with nerves. I turn around to chat with Ralph, Joe, and Tony, but they've swum over to the snack table.

I'm just about to join them when Mrs. Shelby stops the music and speaks into the microphone. "Okay, everyone, it's time for the dance contest."

Pearl and Cora start squealing.

"The first round is a dance-off," Mrs. Shelby continues. "Will all contestants please swim over to the dance floor. I want you to all start dancing, and if I call your name, it means you're out. I'll keep going until only three acts are left! There are no rules about what kind of dancing you do. This is your chance to freestyle!"

The music begins and I start going through the moves Lola and the Shark Beatz have been teaching me over the last few weeks. I don't want to get a big hammer or anything, but I can tell that everyone's kind of impressed.

"Where'd you learn to dance like that, Harry?" someone shouts.

"Awesome moves, Harry!" Tony calls. Joe waves his tentacles in time and starts glowing pink with excitement.

"Yeah, yeah, very cool," says Ralph, "but can you please hurry up so I can have something to eat!"

"Billy Bullshark, you're out!" Mrs. Shelby calls through the microphone. "And Sarah Shellfish, I'm afraid you're not going to the next round."

I don't look at anyone else, I just keep focusing on my moves.

"Kevin Killerwhale, I'm afraid you're out too," Mrs. Shelby calls. "Kevin, put your teeth away this minute! And come and see me after the competition. There's no need to be such a bad loser! Lacy Lungfish, nice try, but I'm sorry, you're out."

And so it goes.

I keep on dancing—and hoping with every fin on my body that I won't hear

Mrs. Shelby call my name. And then, suddenly, the music goes silent. I keep on dancing, too scared to stop.

"Harry Hammer!" Mrs. Shelby calls, and my heart sinks.

I'm out!

"Oh, man!" I sigh, swimming over to Ralph, Joe, and Tony. I don't know why they're grinning. Some friends they are!

"Don't look so gloomy, Harry," Mrs. Shelby says. "You've made it to the final."

WHHHHAAAAAAAATTTTTTTT?!

I turn around. Only the twins and Rick are left on the dance floor. Ralph, Joe, and Tony start finning and tentacle-ing me on the back. I've done it! I've made it to the next round. It's me against Rick and Pearl and Cora!

"Congratulations, dancers!" Mrs. Shelby cries. "Now it's time for our finalists to perform their individual routines. Pearl and Cora, you're first."

Pearl and Cora fluff up their skirts and start to dance. Although their routine is ballet, it's actually quite good. They twirl and kick and turn in perfect time to the music. As they finish, the crowd goes wild. The twins curtsy and wave as they swim off the dance floor.

"Next up, Rick Reef!" Mrs. Shelby cries.

Rick swims to the center of the dance floor and starts doing the coolest dive-jive I have ever seen. The light bouncing off the glitter-pearl sparkles on his blue-whale shoes and his tail is a blur.

Rick finishes with a fin-stand and an awesome dorsal flip.

It's so good, even I'm clapping!

Then, suddenly, I

feel scared. If I'm not even cooler than Rick and even more graceful than the dolphin twins, that Fintendo is never going to be mine.

I take my Shark Beatz cap and shipwreck bling out of my pocket and put them on. I'm going to have to pull out all the stops.

And that means I'm going to have to do my signature move—the immense Hammerhead Head-Spin!

The music booms out. I start busting every move that Lola and the Shark Beatz have drilled into me.

"Go, Harry!" Ralph yells.

"Come on!" Joe and Tony shout, clapping their tentacles and fins in time.

I am a ship-hop king! Just like Moby the Eighth (but better at dancing and without all the headless wives). The light from the glitter-pearl starts bouncing off my bling and reflecting all around the room. I start Six-Tailing in circles across the floor. My cap is on backward and my tracksuit is flapping. The music gets faster. I'm Plopping. I'm Docking. I Drop better than I ever have before. The crowd is clapping along. Whooping and yelling.

I am ON FIRE.

One last Treasure-Chest Pop into the

111

coolest Catfish Daddy and I'm upside-down and ready! The Head-Spin starts out well and the gym becomes a blur as I spin faster. But then something terrible happens. . . .

1. My hammer twists the water around me like a ship's propeller . . .
2. In the skate park, this only twirled the spectators around with it . . .
3. But in the closed space of the gym . . . IT'S A DISASTER!

4. CRASH! ARRRRRRRRRRRGH! SPLAT!
SMASH! OOOOOOOOOOHHHHH!
BOING! FLUBBBERRRRRRRRRRRRRR!!!
KERRRRRRRRRRRRRRUNCH!!!!!!!!!!

By the time the room stops spinning,
everyone is covered in food. And the
boy fish are twisted up with the girl fish.
Awkward.

Mrs. Shelby's glasses are upside-down
and the rest of the teachers are downside-up.
Pearl is somehow wearing Rick's leather
jacket, and Rick is floating backward trying to
get his tail out of her pink skirt.

Joe and Tony are stuck to the ceiling,

clinging to the glitter-pearl for dear life. Ralph is the only one who seems to be okay. He's been flung into the center of a huge cake and is now happily eating his way out of it.

But I'm right in the middle of the devastation—my hammer still vibrating from the worst self-induced flubber of all time.

Mrs. Shelby staggers out from behind the DJ stand. The other teachers start helping everyone untangle themselves from one another, and wipe the food off their faces.

"HARRY!" Mrs. Shelby yells in her sternest voice. "HARRY!"

"Y-y-y-yes, Mrs. Shelby?"

"You are . . . " Mrs. Shelby pauses to

put her glasses back the right way up.

"Y-y-y-y-yes, Mrs. Shelby?"

"You are DISQUALIFIED!"

I hang my hammer in shame.

"Tonight's winners are Pearl and Cora," Mrs. Shelby says.

Rick lets out a loud boo.

"And it is with great pleasure that

I present you with this prize of a Fin-tendo SeaWii-DS!"

I'm all ready for this to be the worst moment of my life ever. But then I see the Fintendo. It's pink and glittery and TOTALLY GIRLY.

My Head-Spin may have wrecked the gym, but it gave me the luckiest escape in gaming history. Rick would have made my life misery if I'd won THAT!

And anyway, I might not have a Fintendo, but at least I've passed my exams and won't have to do any more cramming for a very long time. I've got the whole summer vaca-tion ahead of me to hang out with my best buddies. And I'll be able to see lots more of

 my new friends Lola and the Shark Beatz. No, things aren't too bad after all!

When I get home, the house is very quiet. Mom and Dad must be out at some boring event or they've already gone to bed.

My bedroom door is open, but it's dark inside. "Lenny, can I have some light, please," I call to my lantern fish as I swim inside. Nothing happens. I hope I don't have to change his bulb again—it's so tricky and I always get covered in lantern-fish snot.

"SURPRISE!!!!!!!!!!!!!!!!!!!!!!!!!!!"

I nearly jump out of my skin as the room is flooded with light. Mom and Dad are standing in the middle of the room, with Humphrey and Lenny. All of them have the biggest smiles on their faces.

"We wanted to give you a special surprise, Harry," Mom says. "To say, 'Well done' for passing your exams and working so hard on your studying."

"Yes," says Dad, "we're very impressed with how seriously you've taken your studies."

Mom laughs. "And to

think I was worried that all you wanted to do was play with a Fintendo!"

I put on my most serious face and shake my head.

"So, to say thank-you for all your hard work . . ." Mom says, pulling a box out from behind her, "we've bought you this!"

When I see what's on the box, I almost faint in shock. It's a Fintendo!

I can't believe it. I open the box, with trembling fins. Instead of a pink, glittery, GIRLY Fintendo, there's a brilliant blue, awesomely shiny Fintendo—complete with lots of games!

AMAZING!!!!!!!!!!!!!!!!!!!!!!!!!!

I'm so happy I even hug Mom and Dad without feeling embarrassed. After they leave the room, I high-fin Humphrey and Lenny.

"Still think your mom is an evil dictator, Harry?" laughs Humphrey.

But I don't have time to answer.

I'm too busy firing up Super Snapper Races 8!

THE END

HARRY

Species:

hammerhead shark

You'll spot him . . .

using his special

hammer-vision

Favorite thing:

his Gregor the Gnasher

poster

Most likely to say:

"I wish I was a great white."

Most embarrassing moment: when Mom called him

her "little starfish" in front of all his friends

RALPH

Species:

pilot fish

You'll spot him . . .

eating the food from

between

Harry's teeth!

Favorite thing: shrimp Pop-Tarts

Most likely to say: "So, Harry, what's for

breakfast today?"

Most embarrassing moment: eating too much cake

on Joe's birthday. His face was COVERED in pink

plankton icing.

JOE

Species: jellyfish

You'll spot him . . . hiding behind Ralph and Harry, or behind his own tentacles

Favorite thing: his cave, since it's nice and safe

Most likely to say: "If we do this, we're going to end up as fish food. . . ."

Most embarrassing moment: whenever his rear goes *toot*, which is when he's scared. Which is all the time.

RICK

Species: blacktip reef shark

You'll spot him . . . bullying smaller fish or showing off

Favorite thing: his black leather jacket

Most likely to say: "Last one there's a sea snail!"

Most embarrassing moment: none. Rick's far too cool to get embarrassed.